D1415534

Rabbits In Trouble!

Rabbits In Trouble!

Ana Rosa Marti
Adapted by Judy Grosset
Illustrated by Carmelo Garmendia

First published in this edition 1991
© Peter Haddock Limited
ISBN 0 7105 0605 8
Printed in USSR

Contents

Sick Tricks

Grey Ears woke up one morning to find Brown Ears standing by the side of the bed looking exceedingly grumpy.

"Good morning, Brown Ears. Why the grumpy face on such a fine day?" he asked, stretching and yawning.

"There's no dandelion tea for breakfast, and I suppose it's my turn to go and get it!" grumbled Brown Ears. "I suppose it's my turn, because it always seems to be my turn, and that's why I'm grumpy!"

"Oh don't be so silly!" scolded Grey Ears. "As a matter of fact it is your turn as I have done the shopping for the last three days in a row, but seeing as it is such a beautiful morning, I shall spare you the bother and go for the dandelion tea myself!" With that, Grey Ears cheerily hopped out of bed, put on his clothes, and marched off to the shops.

After he had gone, Brown Ears cheered up considerably. He was really quite a lazy little rabbit, and it was nice to be saved the effort of trailing to the shops. It was nice to have a friend to run after him. It was just a pity that Grey Ears didn't do what Brown Ears wanted all the time. As he was thinking this, a plan was forming in his head. His nose twitched with delight at the very thought. He could get Grey Ears to run around after him, seeing to his every need! All that it would take was a little bit of acting.

Hastily he rummaged in his bedroom cupboard until he found a great big old woolly blanket.

Then he moved his favourite armchair right next to the stove, as close as it would go, and stoked up the stove until it was roasting hot. After a little bit of posing and practising in front of the mirror, he wrapped himself in the blanket, settled himself comfortably in the armchair, and waited for Grey Ears to come back from the shops.

14

When Grey Ears returned a little while later, he found a very different Brown Ears to the one he had spoken to only minutes before.   This Brown Ears was sitting huddled by the stove, wrapped in blankets, with a very sorry expression indeed on his face.

"What on earth is the matter with you, Brown Ears?" he asked in surprise.

"I'm ill, Grey Ears," answered his friend flatly "And I'm afraid I'm
going to be ill for at least a week. I'm afraid that I shall have to rely on
you to look after me – oh, and I'm sorry about the housework. Of
course I would dearly love to help you out, Grey Ears, but I am afraid
that I am simply far too weak. I shall probably need a diet of rich and
nourishing food, in fact, to aid my recovery. Oh, how my head aches!
Could you go and get my breakfast for me, Grey Ears, before I faint?"

Grey Ears meekly left the room and went into the kitchen to prepare
breakfast, without a word of argument.

Brown Ears settled himself comfortably in his chair and smiled.

This was a marvellous game to play!

However, Brown Ears did not realise just how well his little friend
knew him. Through in the kitchen, Grey Ears was quietly preparing
breakfast for Brown Ears, but at the same time he was working out how
to beat Brown Ears at his own game. He knew full well that Brown
Ears was not ill at all!

Seeing Maurice Mouse passing by the window, he popped out and
asked him to call round at Dr Squirrel's surgery and ask him to pay a
visit to the rabbits' house. "Ill for at least a week, eh?" he said to
himself. "We'll soon see about that!"

Dr Squirrel soon arrived, looking very smart indeed in the shiny top
hat which he used for calling upon patients. Grey Ears met him at the
door.

Now to set about his revenge! Brown Ears was really rather scared
of Dr. Squirrel, and Grey Ears knew this very well. Grey Ears was
going to enlist Dr Squirrel's help in making life a lot less easy for the
invalid Brown Ears!

"Thank you for coming, Dr Squirrel," he said. "I don't know if you
will like what I have to say to you.   Brown Ears tells me that he is
feeling very ill, you see, but I am afraid that I simply don't believe him.
Do you think you could take a look at him for me?   I could do with
your assistance!"

Dr Squirrel smiled kindly at Grey Ears.   He, too, knew Brown Ears
and his tricks of old.   "Don't worry, Grey Ears," he said. "Whether
Brown Ears is truly ill or not, I think I shall be able to treat him!"

Brown Ears wasn't too happy to see Dr Squirrel at all.

"I think I am a bit too weak to be bothered with a medical examination!" he protested. "Anyone can see I'm ill, after all!"

"Quiet please, Brown Ears, and breathe in deeply!" ordered Dr Squirrel, pressing his stethoscope to Brown Ears' chest.

"I'm sure I'll have you up and about in a couple of days!" he declared when he had finished his examination.

"Oh, Doctor, I'm sure it will take longer than that!" argued Brown Ears. "I am most dreadfully ill!"

"Oh well, we will see," said Dr. Squirrel. "Now, if you will excuse me, I must discuss your treatment with your friend Grey Ears." And with that he left the room.

"Grey Ears," he said when he got out of the room, "I think a little get-Brown-Ears-to-stop-play-acting treatment is required. This is what I would like you to do"

Dr Squirrel bent down and whispered a series of instructions in Grey Ear's ear. As he whispered, he could see a smile spreading across Grey Ear's face. Grey Ears liked the sound of the doctor's plans!

When he bid goodbye to Dr Squirrel, Grey Ears was giggling in anticipation of the fun that lay ahead of him.

Meanwhile, upstairs in the bedroom, Brown Ears lay back in bed, contented, relaxed and completely unaware of the plotting between Grey Ears and Dr Squirrel down below. He was looking forward to living a life of luxury for several days!

At lunchtime Grey Ears was very busy indeed in the bedroom with Brown Ears. First, he placed a boiling hot-water bottle at his friend's feet, and a painfully cold ice-pack on his head. Then he gave him three different kinds of medicine, two large spoonfuls of each, and each one absolutely disgusting. Finally, he fed Brown Ears a large plateful of cold cucumber and nasturtium soup, which Brown Ears particularly hated.

"Grey Ears, why are you doing this to me?" he cried. "I need proper good food, like apple pies, and carrot soup, and elderberry wine! This ice-pack is killing me, and the hot-water bottle is far too hot! How can I possibly get better if I'm not looked after properly?"

"Oh Brown Ears, can't you see that I am looking after you properly? It's doctor's orders! Lots of medicine, hot feet, cold head, no rich food, and you'll be better in no time!" Grey Ears was enjoying this!

Much to Brown Ears' dismay, it was much the same at teatime. His head ached from all the ice-packs, and his feet tingled terribly from all the hot-water bottles. The medicine still tasted absolutely dreadful, and worst of all, he had to drink two platefuls of cucumber and nasturtium soup! He went to sleep that night feeling very miserable indeed. His plan didn't seem to be working at all well, and he just couldn't work out why.

Grey Ears smiled contentedly to himself as he tucked himself in for the night. One way or another, Brown Ears was going to learn his lesson!

Next morning Grey Ears hopped out of bed happily and went straight into the kitchen to prepare Brown Ears' treatment.

"No breakfast," Dr Squirrel had said. "Just medicine and ice-packs!" Grey Ears prepared the tray and went in to see Brown Ears.

"Where's my breakfast?" demanded Brown Ears.

"No breakfast today!" announced Grey Ears and repeated Dr Squirrel's orders to his friend.

At this, Brown Ears decided that he had had enough, and leapt out
of bed with such force that Grey Ears got quite a fright.

"Right, that's it!" he declared. "I am going to see Dr Squirrel about
this!"

Grey Ears had a little giggle to himself behind Brown Ears' back.
But he did not have long to laugh, because Brown Ears was in action at
once.

Angrily, he struggled into his clothes. "I'll tell that doctor just what I
think of him!" he fumed. "What a way to treat a rabbit who's supposed
to be sick!"

Grey Ears found it hard to conceal his amusement at all this. He
knew that Dr Squirrel had found just the right way to treat Brown Ears,
but he didn't dare tell that to Brown Ears!

23

"Wait for me, Brown Ears!" he called as he ran after his friend down the stairs. "Surely you shouldn't be rushing around like that in your condition!" Grey Ears could hardly keep up for trying not to laugh!

"I am going to see Dr Squirrel *right now,* and I shall give him a piece of my mind!" yelled back Brown Ears.

In no time at all, they had reached Dr Squirrel's surgery.

"Hello there, Brown Ears!" the Doctor greeted them. "It's wonderful to see you here. Didn't I tell you that I would have you up and about in no time?" He winked at Grey Ears. Brown Ears saw the wink, and all of a sudden the truth dawned on him. "Dr Squirrel! Grey Ears! You tricked me! All that horrible medicine – those freezing cold ice-packs – starving me half to death – it was all a trick!"

Dr. Squirrel had hardly time to bid farewell to the two little rabbits as Brown Ears chased Grey Ears out into the street.

"You shouldn't be running so fast in your condition, Brown Ears!" he joked as the two rabbits raced off into the distance.

Up and down the streets Brown Ears chased Grey Ears in his fury. "How could you do this to me, Grey Ears?" he yelled. "That was a dreadful trick to play on me! I thought you were my friend – wait until I catch up with you – I'll pay you back!"

"You started it, Brown Ears!" shouted back Grey Ears. "You pretended to be ill! You tried to trick me into being your slave for a week! You deserved it!"

All the time they were running they kept up the argument, but gradually as they got more and more out of breath, they yelled less and less at each other. When they finally came to a halt, completely breathless, Brown Ears' fury had abated and he could see the funny side of things.

As they puffed and panted, trying to get their breath back, the rabbits suddenly realised that they were standing outside the baker's shop.

This was a favourite place of both Grey Ears and Brown Ears. The rabbits would often stop at this window on their way through the village, and gaze in with mouths watering. The window was always jam–packed full of sticky, gooey, stodgy cakes. And so they gazed again today, their fury with each other forgotten for a moment as they took in the glorious display of goodies before their eyes.

"Don't those cakes look good?" Grey Ears asked his friend.

"Mmm – yes – that big pink sticky one looks the tastiest of all to me! And look at that lovely crusty bread!" Brown Ears remembered just how hungry he was, having had nothing to eat the day before except for medicine and cold cucumber and nasturtium soup. His tummy rumbled and his mouth began to water at the sight of all that delicious food.

It seemed a shame to carry on fighting, when it was much, much nicer to look at the food in friendly companionship. Both rabbits stood for a while in silence, wondering which one would be the first to make friends again, but not quite willing to be the only one to apologise!

Finally Grey Ears turned to his friend and said, "I'll tell you what, Brown Ears. I'll say sorry to you, if you'll say sorry to me!"

Brown Ears thought about this for a moment, "I think that's probably a good idea, Grey Ears," he agreed, "and then we can be friends again."

The two rabbits solemnly shook paws with each other and said sorry to each other most graciously.

"There's one more thing we should do to further seal our renewed friendship, Grey Ears," said Brown Ears very seriously.

"Oh, what's that?" asked Grey Ears. Brown Ears laughed.

"We should have a big sticky bun each – and *you're paying*!" he cried, dragging his friend into the baker's shop with him.

A Fair Frolic

It was the first day of the fair's visit, and Mr Hedgehog was getting ready to go along and see the fun.

He was wearing his best jacket and bow tie, and had his watch and chain on his waistcoat.

He admired himself in the mirror, checked his watch and set off for the fairground.

The fair only came to the village once a year, and it was quite an occasion for everyone.

As he walked along the High Street Mr Hedgehog thought of all the stalls, and of the prizes he might win.   He had saved up all year so that he could afford to try everything.

He loved the excitement of it all – the noise, the hustle and bustle, the smell of food cooking in the open air, the brightly coloured sideshows, and the sticky feel of candy floss on his whiskers.

He felt sure he was going to have a wonderful day.

Poor Harry Hedgehog!   Little did he know what lay in store for him!

And what of Grey Ears and Brown Ears?

At just about the same time, the two rabbits were also on their way to the fair from the other side of the village, but, as usual they didn't have any spending money.

"Listen," said Brown Ears to his friend. "I've got a great plan – why don't we try and earn some money at the fair?"

"Don't be silly," said Grey Ears. "You need a stall with games or something to sell; we don't have anything."

"We could try and get a job!" said Brown Ears. And when they had reached the fairground, he went off to find the fair owner.

He hunted around the stalls and tents without any success, but as he walked, his determination increased. The smell of food wafted all around him and was making him extremely hungry.

He had to make some money to buy some food.

And he had to try some of these games and rides!

He decided to ask some of the stall holders if they knew where he could find the owner.

"Excuse me," he said to the weasels at the entrance. "Have you seen the owner anywhere?"

"Look behind the big tent – you'll see him there."

Brown Ears grabbed Grey Ears and they went to find the owner together.

Brown Ears and Grey Ears were asking the owner if they could work at the fair, when Harry Hedgehog arrived, eager to begin his fun.

"One of the stalls hasn't arrived," said the owner. "Why don't you think of something to take its place?"

Brown Ears caught sight of Harry, and had an idea.

He whispered in Grey Ears' ear, "Just do everything I say, okay?"
and winked.   Grey Ears nodded.

Brown Ears turned to the fair owner.   "Leave it to us, sir!" he said
confidently.

Then he turned to Harry.   "If you'll just help us for five minutes,
Harry, we'll let you try our sideshow for free!"

"Okay then!" Harry agreed.

Brown Ears winked at Grey Ears once more, and they set off to find
their stall with the unsuspecting hedgehog in tow.

With Harry Hedgehog's help, the two rabbits found a bench, two buckets of water, and some sponges in baskets.

"What's all this for?" asked Harry.

"Oh, you'll see in a minute!" said Brown Ears.   He took Grey Ears aside for a moment and whispered to him.   Grey Ears giggled.

"I'll be back," said Brown Ears out loud to Grey Ears.   "I've got an idea – you take Mr Hedgehog and wait for me behind the tent."

Grey Ears and Mr Hedgehog watched Brown Ears run off, and they waited behind the tent.   Then it was Grey Ears' turn to disappear.

"I'll go and find a table to use for our stall – you stay here – sit down over there.," said Grey Ears pointing, to the bench.

37

Poor, poor Harry!   He had no idea at all that he was about to be used so cruelly.   Content with the thought that he was going to have a free shot on this mysterious sideshow in return for his help, he obediently sat down to wait on the bench as he had been told to do.

The rabbits seemed to be away for a long time, so Mr Hedgehog settled down to read a newspaper which had been lying on the bench. He had just turned to the horoscopes when *suddenly* . . . .

"*Roll up, roll up* – hit the hedgehog – win a prize!" Mr Hedgehog recognised Brown Ears' voice.

"What the . . . !!" exclaimed Mr Hedgehog.   He was being assaulted by soggy sponges!

Mr Hedgehog looked up – he couldn't believe his eyes.   Someone was throwing the sponges at him.

Constable Weasel was enjoying himself immensely, having a wonderful time.

Harry Hedgehog was not having a wonderful time, however. He was by now soaking wet from head to toe. His best jacket was positively dripping, and he could feel the water soaking right through to his underwear.

How would you feel if it had happened to you?

Mr Hedgehog was furious. He jumped up from his seat and immediately he started to throw the sponges back at Constable Weasel.

"Aah!" yelled Constable Weasel as the first sponge hit him full in the face.

"Bleh!" he spluttered as another sponge knocked his hat off, sending water cascading down the back of his neck.

"*Stop!*" he yelled, just in time to stop Harry Hedgehog from throwing another sponge at him.

Now, up until Constable Weasel shouted "*Stop*", Harry Hedgehog had been too angry to see who he had been throwing the sponges at. He had merely been throwing them in a blind rage, getting revenge for his own soaking. All of a sudden, he realised who it was that he had been taking out his anger upon. Poor Harry Hedgehog! He was so embarrassed and frightened that he would be in trouble with Constable Weasel. He turned to run away, but Constable Weasel caught him firmly by the sleeve of his jacket. Harry Hedgehog quaked with fear at what might happen to him now, but he need not have worried.

Constable Weasel had thought that he had been throwing sponges at a dummy! When he realised that it was Harry Hedgehog, and that Harry Hedgehog was not expecting to have sponges thrown at him, Constable Weasel had swiftly worked out what had happened.

"BROWN EARS AND GREY EARS!" he roared at the top of his voice.

Brown Ears and Grey Ears fled.

The rabbits ran for their lives, chased by Constable Weasel and a very angry Mr Hedgehog, who were armed with sponges which they were aiming at the rabbits.

"Faster," yelled Grey Ears. "They're catching up."

And so ended the rabbits' day at the fair.   They ran without stopping until they reached the safety of their own little house.   There they stayed, having earned no money and having had not a single go at any of the sideshows.

And what of the others?   After a while they gave up chasing Grey Ears and Brown Ears.   They had given the rascally pair a good fright, and that was enough.

Harry Hedgehog and Constable Weasel went home to change into dry clothes, and then they went back to join the rest of the village animals, enjoying all the fun of the fair.

Mr Badger
And The Carrots

One morning, Grey Ears woke up to find that his friend was already up and about and in a happy mood.

"Come on, wake up, sleepy head!" said Brown Ears.

"Oh? What time is it?" asked Grey Ears sleepily.

"It's late, and time to get up."

"What's for breakfast?" yawned Grey Ears, sitting up in bed.

"What do you mean, 'What's for breakfast?' You know there is no food in the house. When do we ever have food in the house? – I'm starving!" complained Brown Ears.

"What are we going to do?" wailed Grey Ears.

"We'll have to find some work to earn enough money to fill the larder," said Brown Ears.

"But who's going to give us work after all the trouble we've caused?"

Brown Ears looked seriously at his friend. "There's nothing else for it. We'll have to turn over a new leaf. We'll have to do a few good turns and persuade people to trust us," he said.

Grey Ears looked thoughtful. "Mm," he said. "I suppose it's worth a try."

The two friends got dressed and went out. The village was bustling.
Everyone was hurrying to work, except of course the two rabbits, who
could only stand and watch.

"I bet they've all had breakfast," moaned Grey Ears.

The two rabbits stood for quite a while watching the world go by.

Neither of them had ever had what you would call a proper job.

They didn't know what it was like to get up early and work all day and every day.

"Why don't you get a proper job, Brown Ears?" said Grey Ears thoughtfully.   "Then we would have enough money to live on without having to come up with clever schemes all the time."

"Why don't you get a job?" replied Brown Ears.

"You're much cleverer than I am.   You're the one with all the ideas. You'd be much better at a proper job than I would."

The truth was that both rabbits were equally lazy and equally reluctant to try to find regular work.   They had grown so used to their way of life that they would find it very difficult to change.

They spent every day wondering where their next meal was coming from, and the whole village knew it, and everyone was very, very wary of the two rabbits, who were becoming really quite unpopular with their wily ways.

Nobody would lend them anything, because they knew that they would be highly unlikely to get it back.

Nobody would trust them, for at some time or another practically everybody in the village had suffered some form of misfortune at the hands of the rascally pair.

And even when, as so often happened, the two rabbits were penniless and hungry, the other animals were unwilling to help, as they felt that Grey Ears' and Brown Ears' predicament was their own fault.

Just then, Mr Badger went past carrying a sack. A very heavy sack by the look of it, because he was walking very slowly, bent under the weight of his load.

"I know!" whispered Grey Ears softly. "We could offer to carry Mr Badger's load!"

"What a good idea," agreed Brown Ears. "Quick! I know a short cut. We'll get ahead of him. Then we can catch him when he's really tired and willing to let us help."

The rabbits set off.   Their plan was to meet Mr Badger further up the
road.   They were sure that he hadn't noticed them standing watching
him earlier.   They ran as fast as they could, remembering all the tricks
they had played on Mr Badger in the past.

"I hope he doesn't hold any grudges against us," panted Grey Ears as they ran.

"We'll soon find out," puffed Brown Ears breathlessly.

They rounded the next corner, jumped over a fence and ran to the edge of the road that Mr Badger would be coming along very soon.

Brown Ears had been thinking to himself as they ran that he did not relish the thought of carrying that heavy sack, and as they reached the road and sat by a tree waiting for Mr Badger, he said to Grey Ears, "I think it would be best if you helped Mr Badger today.   After all, he has only one sack to carry.   There's no point in both of us offering to carry one sack is there?"

Grey Ears nodded.   "It won't take long," he said, "You stay here and wait for me, then we can go and tell everyone how helpful we've been."

"All right," said Brown Ears, smiling to himself.

"Careful – here comes Badger now!"

Brown Ears, of course, was willing to trick even his best friend into doing all the hard work for him, but Grey Ears, as usual, had been completely taken in.

Poor Grey Ears!

"Good morning, Mr Badger," said Grey Ears politely. "That looks like a heavy load you're carrying. Can I help you?"

"Well er – good morning, Grey Ears," said a rather surprised Mr Badger. "I would very much like some help, but I'll walk with you as you carry my sack to my house. I don't trust you to deliver it."

"Really, Mr Badger! You mustn't believe all the stories you hear about us. We're really very trustworthy rabbits – aren't we, Brown Ears?" exclaimed Grey Ears as he swung the heavy sack on his shoulders, and set off with Mr Badger.

"See you later!" Brown Ears called as they strode off down the path towards Badger Cottage.

Unknown to Mr Badger and Grey Ears, as the rabbit had lifted the sack from the ground, a carrot had fallen out from a hole in the bottom of it. Brown Ears had spotted it straight away.

Brown Ears waited until Grey Ears and Badger were out of sight. He stared after them and couldn't believe his eyes. There was a trail of carrots all the way down the road!

He went to fetch another sack, which he had spotted at the edge of the field, and hurried back to collect the carrots that had dropped out of the sack, and soon he had a full load.

He did not stop to think that as Grey Ears' load was getting lighter, his own was getting heavier!

He did not even realise that he was actually working; he was too busy thinking of steaming bowls of carrot soup!

Meanwhile, Grey Ears and Mr Badger had nearly reached Badger Cottage when Mr Badger noticed that the sack was nearly empty.

"So this is how you help me!" he roared, picking Grey Ears up by his collar and shaking him hard until his teeth rattled.

"You and your accomplice have plotted together to steal my crop of carrots!"

"I don't know what you mean," shrieked Grey Ears. "Honestly, I've just been trying to help!"

Mr Badger gave up. He was extremely angry. He just couldn't believe that he'd lost so much of his crop of carrots.

It was obvious that Mr Badger wasn't prepared to listen to anything that Grey Ears had to say, so the rabbit saw his chance and ran off just as fast as his frightened legs would carry him.

He had to find Brown Ears and warn him that their plan had failed.

He looked over his shoulder to see if Badger was chasing him, but Mr Badger was just standing there, shaking his fist in fury.

Brown Ears had been having a rest while he waited for his friend. He had hidden the carrots, which he had piled up behind the tree, in case anyone should come along and ask awkward questions.

He was surprised to see Grey Ears back so quickly, as it was really quite a long way to Badger's cottage.

"Quick – hide!" shouted Grey Ears. "It's all gone wrong!"

"What's happened?" asked Brown Ears.

"Badger thinks that you and I plotted to steal his carrots and doesn't believe we were just trying to help!"

"Oh, that's just terrible," said Brown Ears, smiling.

"What's so funny?" said a very puzzled looking Grey Ears. "Now we can't hope to persuade people to give us work so that we can buy food. This is a desperate situation!"

"Is it really?" said Brown Ears. "I don't think we'll be hungry for long!"

He pulled out his sack of carrots and showed it to his astonished friend.

"But – but – how did you get these?" stammered Grey Ears.

"Oh, let's just say that they fell at my feet!" grinned Brown Ears. "Now, come on, let's get home and do some cooking!"

So saying, our cheeky friend took Grey Ears by the arm, swung the sack over his shoulder, and they headed off to savour their ill-gotten gains.

Conversation Piece

The last person in the village who had spoken to Brown Ears was
Constable Weasel, and that had been four whole days ago.   Brown
Ears was in a great deal of trouble.

"Go home, Brown Ears," Constable Weasel had said, "before I am forced to lock you in jail.   And don't set foot in the High Street again until you are prepared to apologise for your behaviour.   There is hardly an animal left in this village who is still prepared to speak to you.   If it weren't for Grey Ears, you wouldn't have any friends left!"

Brown Ears had huffily got up and trudged off home with Grey Ears trailing along behind him.

For two days Brown Ears had stayed at home, seeing nobody but his friend, and sending Grey Ears out to the shops for him whenever he felt hungry.   For two days he had quite enjoyed himself, in fact.   He had plenty of peace and quiet, no boring shopping to do, and lots of time to laze about in the garden in the sunshine.

On the third day, however, the rain had come down in torrents. Brown Ears had been forced to stay inside.   Without the garden and the sunshine to enjoy, Brown Ears was rather at a loss.   He would not, of course, consider doing any housework – he was far too lazy to even think of that!   Grey Ears was quite content to sit in a comfortable armchair and read a book, but even that was too much like work for Brown Ears.   Brown Ears was *bored*.

Ask any grown-up, and they will tell you that when children are bored it often means trouble, for bored children often get up to mischief.

Brown Ears was just like a child in many ways – a bored Brown Ears often meant a naughty Brown Ears.   Grey Ears knew this and was feeling rather anxious!

Brown Ears paced up and down the living room, his nose twitching with impatience.   Then he went over to the window and looked gloomily out.

"I think I'll just put on my coat and splash along to the shops," he said to Grey Ears as he watched the rain dripping and splashing onto the window sill outside. "Just to see if anything is happening, you know!" he added.

"Oh no you don't, Brown Ears!" warned his friend.

"What do you mean?" asked Brown Ears.

"Have you forgotten already?" Grey Ears was surprised. "Constable Weasel has banned you from the High Street until you have apologised for all the mischief you have been causing lately! You can't just forget about what he said and go out! If he sees you when you're out he'll put you in jail for sure!"

"Oh yes, right enough, Grey Ears," said Brown Ears gloomily. "I had almost forgotten about all that. Honestly, what a fuss everybody makes about a jolly creature like me having a harmless bit of fun! You know, Grey Ears, I don't think anybody around here has much of a sense of humour at all!"

Grey Ears looked a little doubtful. He knew just how out of hand Brown Ears' "harmless fun" had become recently.

Brown Ears paced up and down the room restlessly.

Grey Ears watched him, annoyed that he couldn't concentrate on the book that he was trying to read.

Finally Brown Ears stopped pacing, stamped his foot rather crossly, and with a heavy sigh announced:

"So they want an apology, do they? All right then, they'll get one!"

For the rest of the day and almost all evening Brown Ears was busy trying to compose his apology. He found this a particularly hard thing to do because, in fact, he wasn't particularly sorry for what he had done!

Finally, after a short break and something to eat, he settled down for one last try.   He pretended that there was a monster behind him, waiting to swallow him in one gulp if he didn't finish quickly.

His imagination was so good that he made himself really scared and finished writing in three minutes flat!

Then, exhausted, he went to bed.

Next day, bright and early, Brown Ears got up and dressed himself
and marched into the village, carrying a hammer, a large nail, and a
piece of paper.

On the paper he had written in his best writing (which still wasn't very tidy!):

"I, Brown Ears Rabbit, do apologise
most sincerely for all the trouble that
I seem to have caused to the good
citizens of Whiskerton.   I truly did
not mean to be such a nuisance,
nor to make anybody unhappy.
I will try my best to mend my ways
and live the life of a quiet, honest
citizen in the future."

He walked over to the large oak tree in the middle of the High Street and nailed up the piece of paper for all to see.

The other animals in the street all gathered round to have a look.

"Huh! Bet he doesn't mean a word of it!" muttered Mr Mouse to Freddie Fox.

"Lot of rubbish if you ask me!" Toby Turtle remarked to no one in particular.

Without another word, every one of them turned away!

Brown Ears realised that he might be allowed in the High Street now, but in spite of his apology it seemed that the other animals were still not speaking to him.

Something would have to be done.

He set off home, and on his way he met Grey Ears, who had come along to see how his friend had got on with the other villagers.   Brown Ears told him what had happened.   "But not to worry, Grey Ears! I have a plan!"

Grey Ears looked worried for a moment, but Brown Ears was quick to reassure him.

"Don't worry, Grey Ears, I'm not going to do anything dishonest! I'm not going to get us into any trouble! I am simply going to take up a little hobby to pass the time. Now, my dear fellow, would you do me a favour and get a few things from the shops for me?"

Later that morning Harry Hedgehog and Mrs Mouse stopped Grey
Ears in the street.

Grey Ears was carrying an easel, some brushes and a canvas.

"What are these for?" Harry asked.

"Brown Ears," said Grey Ears with a twinkle in his eye, "has taken
up painting."   And off he went home.

Back home, Grey Ears helped his wily chum to set up all his equipment.

"Don't forget to use your artist's palette to mix all your colours properly," he reminded him.

"Don't you worry, Grey Ears, I'll be mixing away like an expert in no time!" his friend beamed. "I think I might even be quite good at this!"

"That may well be true," agreed Grey Ears, "but how is it going to make the other animals start speaking to you again?"

Brown Ears took a deep breath, and adjusted the canvas on his easel.

"All I can say, Grey Ears, is that you will have to wait and see for yourself!"

For the next day and a half Brown Ears spent most of his time outside in the garden, working away at his painting.

He worked very slowly and carefully, spending a long time mixing each colour and painting tiny lines, shapes and patterns on the canvas.

"It's going to take you ages to finish at this rate!" commented Grey Ears. "What is it anyway, Brown Ears?"

"Well, what do you think it is?" said Brown Ears mysteriously.

"I'm sure I don't know!" replied his friend, puzzled. "And I still don't see how you intend to get yourself back in favour with the other villagers!"

"Wait and see, my friend, wait and see," said Brown Ears confidently.

He took a little blob of red paint and drew a tiny squiggle up in the right hand corner of the canvas. Then he stood back for a moment to admire his work.

After some consideration, he put a little green dot beside the red squiggle. Grey Ears watched him with amazement. It was a long time since he had seen his friend concentrating quite so hard as this on anything. The painting was proving to be an absorbing pastime for Brown Ears indeed!

The reason behind it all was still a bit of a mystery to Grey Ears, but he had to admit it was nice to see his friend so happy at his work!

That afternoon, Brown Ears' Uncle Ronald called round. He had heard that Brown Ears had taken up painting and was curious to see how he was getting on. He was so pleasantly surprised to see Brown Ears working so hard that he completely forgot that he wasn't speaking to him.

"I say, Brown Ears!" he exclaimed. "That's a rather nice picture! What is it exactly?"

"What do you think it is?" was all that Brown Ears would say in reply. Grey Ears was now beginning to see exactly what Brown Ears was up to!

Next morning dawned bright and sunny, and Brown Ears set up his easel in the garden once more, and carried on with his painting. Mrs Duck from the Post Office appeared behind him, peering with great interest at his work. Harry Hedgehog had indeed been spreading the news about Brown Ears' new hobby!

Just as Uncle Ronald had done, Mrs Duck opened her beak to speak to Brown Ears before she realised what she was doing.

"Oh my, Brown Ears!" she quacked. "What wonderful colours you are using in that picture. It makes me feel happy just looking at it!"

"Why, thank you, Mrs Duck," replied Brown Ears modestly.

"What are you going to call it? Is it supposed to be something, or is it an abstract?"

"Oh Mrs Duck, I'm afraid I must leave you wondering for the moment," said Brown Ears with a knowing wink, "but perhaps you will be able to understand the picture better when it's finished."

"Yes, yes, perhaps I will," agreed Mrs Duck, "but whatever it is, Brown Ears, I have to say that I think it's very pretty indeed!"

And off she waddled, having completely forgotten that Brown Ears was supposed to be out of favour.

If Harry Hedgehog had done well spreading the news about Brown Ears and his artwork, then Mrs Duck did twice as well. Mrs Duck owned the Post Office in Whiskerton. It was one of the busiest places in the village, and every animal who came in to do some business at the Post Office that day was told about Brown Ears' painting. "You mean you spoke to Brown Ears?" someone asked. "I thought that we were not going to speak to him until we were sure that he was going to change his ways!"

Mrs Duck was quick to defend herself. "Oh, I'm sure he has been behaving himself. He has been working so hard on that picture that he hasn't had time to get up to any mischief. And it's such a pretty picture – oh I wish I knew what it was supposed to be!"

Everybody now became curious to see Brown Ears' work for themselves. All anger with him seemed to be forgotten as the villagers vied with each other to guess what the picture was, or at least what it was meant to be. And, as it turned out, most of the animals liked the painting! From then on Brown Ears had a constant stream of visitors to the garden "studio".

Constable Weasel came along with Mrs Squirrel and Mrs Mole that afternoon. He was surprisingly impressed with what he saw. "Very nice, Brown Ears, very nice indeed!" he found himself saying.

"Why, thank you, Constable Weasel! That's just about the nicest thing you've ever said to me!" exclaimed Brown Ears.

"Can't begin to think what you might call it though," admitted Constable Weasel.

"You'll find out sooner or later!" beamed Brown Ears.

Sammy Squirrel and Mrs Mouse were the next to call upon the artist. Mrs Mouse had plenty of ideas about what the painting was supposed to be, but Brown Ears firmly told her that she was completely wrong. Poor Mrs Mouse!   She was really quite cross.   She hated secrets, and this secret was one which particularly irritated her!

Sammy Squirrel said very little, but looked at the picture very admiringly indeed.

This particularly pleased Brown Ears for Sammy Squirrel, just like his uncle, Dr Squirrel, was a very clever animal with good taste.

For him to like Brown Ears' painting was quite a compliment!

And so it went on all afternoon, and all the next day; visitor after visitor called at the rabbits' house.   Grey Ears was amazed at how well Brown Ears' plan had worked.   Brown Ears had been very clever indeed.   All the villagers had put all thought of Brown Ears' previous bad behaviour completely out of their heads.   Only two days ago they would have avoided speaking to him at all costs – today they were crowding in to see him and talk to him.

Brown Ears had realised that curiosity is a powerful thing!

The mystery of the painting, and what it was meant to be, had aroused everybody's curiosity.   Everybody wanted to know the answer, and a lot of the animals thought they might have it.   "Is it a tree in blossom?" asked one.

"Don't be silly!   It has no trunk!" said another.

"Is it a picture of a dream that you have had?" asked somebody else.

Brown Ears gave nothing away, but kept on painting, slowly and carefully, a dab here, a splash there, all the time smiling secretly to himself.

The arguments among the onlookers went on around him as his painting slowly progressed.   Brown Ears was very careful not to paint too fast, however, because he didn't want to finish while the visitors were still there.   You see not even Brown Ears knew what he was painting – he had only started the picture to get people to talk to him again.   He hadn't thought of a title for it at all!

Late that evening, when the last of the visitors had gone, Brown Ears put the finishing touches to his painting and sat down in a chair to survey his handiwork.   He was rather proud of his efforts; it was a nice painting, full of rich colour and intricate pattern.   "I wonder what I will call it?" he thought idly to himself.   But all the fresh air and all the work and all the visitors had taken their toll.   He was too tired to think. He was too tired to move!   He fell asleep right where he was, in the chair in the garden.

"Luckily it didn't rain during the night!" Brown Ears was woken next morning by the voice of Harry Hedgehog. "It would have ruined your lovely painting! Sorry if I disturbed you, but I just wanted to ask you if you would be willing to sell it to me! I know just the spot where I could hang that picture in my house!"

Brown Ears was delighted. He had never dreamt that anyone would want to buy his picture!

Harry toddled off to get some vegetables and money to pay for it.

"This has worked out even better than I could have imagined!"
Brown Ears told Grey Ears when Harry had gone.   "I haven't been in
trouble for days, everybody is friends with me again, and I am going to
earn some money!"

Grey Ears was delighted for his friend.

"Don't forget to sign the painting like a true artist!" he reminded him.

"Righto!" said Brown Ears and signed with a flourish.

A Little while later, a very pleased Harry Hedgehog came to take possession of his new picture.   In return he gave Brown Ears half a dozen beautiful cabbages, some carrots and five pound coins.

"By the way, Brown Ears, what is the painting called?" he asked before he set off for home.

"After some thought, Harry, I have decided not to give it a name as such.   Let's just say it's a conversation piece!" said Brown Ears, laughter in his eyes.

Brown Ears was back in favour with the villagers – but for how long, I wonder?

And what of his painting?   Well, he did do more paintings from time to time when he needed some peace and quiet, or when he found himself at a loose end.   Some were good enough to sell, some he gave away as presents, but none quite managed to match up to his first, great Conversation Piece!

Missing

One morning Grey Ears decided to take a walk through the forest to
the next village to see his grandmother.

"Make sure she gives you something nice to bring home for supper!"
joked Brown Ears.

"That's not funny, Brown Ears!" scolded his friend. "You know that
my grandmother is very poor. It would be quite wrong to take food
from her!"

"I'm sorry, Grey Ears," said Brown Ears. "I didn't really mean it."

A little while later, Brown Ears waved his friend goodbye at the front door.   Grey Ears was looking very smart indeed, wearing his very best clothes, all neatly pressed, and his Sunday hat was ready to be perched neatly between two well-scrubbed ears.

"Goodbye, Brown Ears!" he called cheerily as he set off down the street.   "I should be back quite soon after lunch.   Grandmother gets tired easily so I don't want to stay too long with her."

Off he set through the village, feeling rather proud of himself in his smart outfit. Everybody he passed noticed that he was looking unusually neat and tidy. "Why, Grey Ears!" they exclaimed. "We can hardly recognise you! What are you and Brown Ears up to this time?"

"Nothing!" retorted Grey Ears. "I'm going to visit my grandmother in the village beyond the forest, and I want her to see me looking my very best!"

But Constable Weasel was suspicious of Grey Ears.   He followed
him quite a long way along the road, writing things in his notebook and
asking questions in a loud cross voice. "I don't trust you and your
friend, Grey Ears! Where are you going?   Why are you going there?
How do I know whether you are telling me the truth?"   Grey Ears
thought he would never be able to get away, but at the edge of the
forest Constable Weasel finally gave up to let him carry on by himself.

It was quite a long walk through the forest for Grey Ears, but it was a lovely day and he enjoyed listening to the birdsong in the trees above his head, and smelling the sweet scent of the honeysuckle and wild roses which were dotted here and there among the many shrubs and bushes along the way.   All the same, he was a little nervous at the thought of his return journey.   His grandmother did so like to chat, and if she kept him talking too long, then Grey Ears would have to walk back home in the dark.   The forest was quite spooky at night, so Grey Ears hoped he would get away from his grandmother in time to avoid going through it in the darkness.

Back in the village, Brown Ears spent a very quiet morning.   After a delicious lunch of carrot stew, he sat down in his favourite armchair and closed his eyes for a little rest – just long enough to let his lunch settle properly in his tummy, he thought to himself.   He didn't have a little rest – he had a very big rest! In fact, he fell fast asleep in that armchair and snored his furry little head off until it was nearly time for tea.

He woke up, feeling a rumbling in his tummy that told him it was time for some food, and he looked around for Grey Ears.   There was no sign of him.

"He should be back home by now," thought Brown Ears, and he set off to see if Grey Ears had stopped somewhere in the village on his way home.   He wanted to know why his friend was late.

Outside in the street Brown Ears asked all the villagers he met whether they had seen Grey Ears that afternoon.   They had all seen Grey Ears in the morning, resplendent in his best clothes on his way to his grandmother's, but not one of them had seen him coming back. Brown Ears began to get a little worried.

"Perhaps he's popped in to see Mrs Mole on his way home." Brown Ears thought to himself. Brown Ears and Grey Ears often called into Mrs Mole's for a visit. She was renowned in Whiskerton for her wonderful cooking, and the two rabbits were always hoping for a taste of whatever dish she was preparing. There was just a chance that, finding himself hungry after his journey, Grey Ears had called at Mrs Mole's in the hope that there might be a spare tasty morsel for him to nibble.

However, when Brown Ears got to Mrs Mole's house he was disappointed. There was no sign of Grey Ears. Brown Ears then tried Mrs Squirrel's sweet shop and Harry Hedgehog's allotment, where Grey Ears often went when he was hungry, but with no luck.

This was a real problem. Grey Ears was never late home. Like Brown Ears, he was always hungry and would not want to miss his tea or his supper. It was getting late now, and soon it would be dark. There was only one answer: something terrible must have happened to Grey Ears. Brown Ears must get help immediately.

"I think Grey Ears may be lost – perhaps even kidnapped!" he exclaimed to the villagers. "I need some people to help me come and look for him. Can any of you come?"

"Ha, ha, Brown Ears!" they retorted. "You've tried tricks like this before! Don't think you can fool us so easily this time! Go and play your joke on somebody else!"

It was the same everywhere that Brown Ears went. Nobody
believed him. Some people just laughed at him; others became very
angry indeed; and Mrs Duck even slammed the door of her house in
his face.

Poor Brown Ears. He sat down on the pavement and cried. It seemed that after all his tricks and nonsense nobody thought it possible that this time he could be telling the truth. And poor Grey Ears! Lost out there with nobody to find him. Brown Ears would just have to search for his friend all by himself.

He dried his eyes, dusted himself down, and set off in a determined fashion towards the forest. It was getting dark now, and he was feeling a little bit nervous about going into the forest alone, so to keep up his courage he muttered to himself as he went along: "I must find poor Grey Ears. I must find poor Grey Ears." He walked right past Constable Weasel without even noticing him. Constable Weasel saw the tear stains on Brown Ears' face.

"I wonder what's wrong with that rascal?" he said to himself, as he walked on. He came upon a group of villagers and asked them what was the matter with Brown Ears. "Oh, he's trying to pretend that Grey Ears is lost or kidnapped," they scoffed. "Of course, we don't believe him."

"I'm not so sure that he's pretending this time," said Constable Weasel. "It is my duty as a police constable to protect the animals of this village. If this is a joke then of course the rabbits will be in serious trouble. But although it may seem like a nuisance I must go and look for Grey Ears. And I must have some other animals to help me search. The forest is very big, and it is getting darker and darker. Go and get some more animals to help, all of you ! We must set off at once !"

Constable Weasel's words alarmed the villagers. After all, it was certainly true that no one had seen Grey Ears since that morning, and Brown Ears was perhaps genuinely upset.

The two rabbits could be a great nuisance, that was true, but nobody would wish them to come to any harm.

Rosie Rabbit became quite distressed. "Oh, poor Grey Ears!" she wailed.

Mrs Mouse was likewise overcome, and Rosie and she cried bitterly
as the other villagers spread the news of the search.

After a few minutes, a large group of villagers had gathered together. They hurried along the road towards the forest, led by Constable Weasel. Everybody was very worried by now. "Don't worry, I'm sure we'll find Grey Ears soon," he said to comfort them. But by now it was very dark, and even he was a little bit scared.

Suddenly, they heard a funny noise. Everyone stopped. They listened again. A sort of "shuffle" then a quiet "boohoo", and then a rustling! Carefully, they peered over the top of the bushes. What could it be! What a relief! It was only Brown Ears, crying his eyes out, poor rabbit. "Don't cry, Brown Ears, we've come to help you!" they told him, and took him along with them.

They searched behind trees, under bushes, and in every place they could think of. No sign of Grey Ears. They searched until they were nearly too tired to go on searching.

    And then, at last, they heard another noise, coming from some
bushes.

    Constable Weasel shone his torch on the bushes.   There was a pair
of very familiar grey ears sticking out !

    "Grey Ears!" cried Brown Ears, pulling his friend out of the bushes,
and giving him a great big hug.   "What happened to you?

I've been so worried!"

Grey Ears looked very ashamed of himself. He began his explanation:

"I was very nearly home, Brown Ears, when I remembered my hat!"

"Your hat?" interrupted Brown Ears.

"Yes, my hat, Brown Ears. I left it at my grandmother's" house! I was going back to get it, but I wasn't really thinking where I was supposed to be going. I took a wrong turning, and I got lost! Then it got dark, and I got scared, so I just hid in the bushes; I am so glad that you found me!"

The happy band then made their way back to the village.

Next day, after a good night's sleep to recover from their adventure, the two rabbits were out for a stroll.

"You know, Grey Ears," said Brown Ears, "you shouldn't be scared of the dark in the forest. I certainly wasn't!"

Grey Ears believed him.

Do you?

Good Intentions

"What are you reading, Grey Ears?" Brown Ears asked his little friend one evening. Grey Ears had his nose buried deep in a very big and important-looking book.

"This is very interesting, you know," said Grey Ears. "It's a book about old traditions, and this bit is all about New Year's resolutions. They seem like a good idea to me!"

"What are New Year's resolutions then, Grey Ears? Are they a good way to make money or something?" Brown Ears was interested.

His friend shook his head.

"No, no, Brown Ears, nothing like that. Let me explain. At the end of every year, on New Year's Eve, you sit down and make a list of all the things that you have been doing wrong that you want to change."

"Like what?" asked Brown Ears.

"Well, perhaps you are very untidy, or perhaps you eat too many sweet things, or tell lies or have been unkind to somebody. . . ."

"Stop! I see what you mean!" squeaked Brown Ears. He was getting embarrassed by this list of wrongdoing, for he knew well that he was guilty of all these things! Grey Ears looked at Brown Ears very sternly for a moment then continued: "Well, you make a list of all the things, and then you make another list, promising not to do them in the New Year. These promises are New Year's resolutions. Once New Year has come, you try your very best to turn over a new leaf and to keep the resolutions."

"It all sounds a bit like hard work. . ." said Brown Ears thoughtfully.

"Yes," agreed Grey Ears, "but it shows people that you are trying to improve and change your ways. Don't you think it would be nice, Brown Ears, if people really believed that we were making an effort to change our ways and behave ourselves? Just think of all the people in the village who hardly speak to us because of all the things we've done to them in the past; wouldn't it be wonderful if they became our friends again? It's just a pity that it isn't New Year just now, for I can tell you, Brown Ears, some New Year's resolutions might just do us some good!"

Brown Ears nodded thoughtfully, and both rabbits were silent for a moment. Then Brown Ears jumped up excitedly.

"Why wait for New Year? It's Midsummer's Eve tomorrow, isn't it? Let's make some Midsummer's resolutions! Nobody will care that it isn't New Year. They'll just be pleased to hear that we two have turned over a new leaf and are trying to behave for a change! First thing tomorrow, Grey Ears, we'll make our list. Then we'll give out copies all around the village so that everybody knows what good rabbits we're going to be. We'll make friends with everybody again, and everything will be wonderful!"

Grey Ears looked at his friend in delight. Just for once, it looked as if Brown Ears had thought of a plan that wouldn't get them into trouble. It was almost too good to be true!

That night the rabbits slept the sleep of the just, dreaming of the future that awaited them as newly upright and honest citizens of Whiskerton, respected by all the other animals. "Honesty is the best policy," as Grey Ears' Uncle Ronald always used to say, and that night at least, Brown Ears was determined to make the very best effort to follow his Uncle's good advice.

The two rabbits were up at the crack of dawn the next day, making up their list of resolutions.

"Golly, this is hard work, Grey Ears!" said Brown Ears. "I hadn't really thought about it before, but we've done so many things wrong that it takes an awfully long time to write about them all!"

Grey Ears could only agree. The list seemed endless; if they didn't make it shorter in some way, they would never be finished before the end of the day.

In the end they decided to write down only the things that they did most often and resolve not to do them again, and then at the end of

their list of resolutions they wrote: "We both know we are guilty of many other wrongdoings and hereby promise to do our very best not to do any of them again either." Having done that, the two rabbits had completed their list by lunchtime, and had also written out several other copies to stick up around the village for all to see. After a welcome bowl of carrot soup and some lovely crusty bread, they set off to deliver the copies to prominent places in the village.

By mid-afternoon the village was buzzing with excitement. "Just look, Mrs Mole!" exclaimed Mrs Duck at the Post Office, pointing to the list of resolutions newly pinned to her wall in a smart wooden frame. "They've promised never to play with my rubber date stamps again, or to break my parcel weighing scales. Remember how Brown Ears used to sit on them to weigh himself? He's so heavy they broke every time! These resolutions are wonderful news! Now, Mrs Mole, would you please look after the shop for me for a little while? I promised Grey Ears that I would take one of these lists over to Dr Squirrel's house for him!"

Mrs Mole took up position behind the Post Office counter instead of Mrs Duck, and Mrs Duck slipped off upstairs to get ready to go. She was pleased to see Grey Ears and Brown Ears were ready to mend their ways, and she wanted to do something to encourage them.

As she looked in the mirror to check that her new hat was on straight, Mrs Duck had an idea. On her way back from Dr Squirrel's she would deliver a nice apple pie to Grey Ears' and Brown Ears' house. These good intentions deserved to be rewarded, and a tasty pie would make a lovely reward!

Harry Hedgehog, meanwhile, could not believe what he was reading!
He had been given a copy of the rabbits' resolutions to put up outside
the village allotments, and there, fourth item on the list, was written:

"We promise to stop stealing carrots and lettuces or anything else that grows in Harry Hedgehog's allotment."

This was marvellous news – simply marvellous news!

"I think I'll give the rabbits a pound or two of carrots as a gesture of appreciation," he thought to himself. "I know that Brown Ears finds my vegetables particularly tasty."

Outside the Police Station another copy had been pinned to the door, and a crowd had gathered round to read it. "Look here, Constable Weasel, it says that Grey Ears and Brown Ears are going to stop giving you so much extra work to do!" said Percy Pig.

"Well, that's certainly good news if it's true!" replied Constable Weasel. "Life will be much easier for me in the future if these rascals really do mean to behave themselves!" He was so pleased that he rushed home to tell his wife, who made some poppy seed cake for the rabbits immediately as a reward.

And so it went on throughout the afternoon. By teatime the rabbits had quite a selection of goodies in their store cupboard, given by the village people in gratitude for them turning over a new leaf.

"It's lucky for us you read that book last night, Grey Ears!" exclaimed Brown Ears. "Who gave the book to you?"

"Oh, Rosie Rabbit lent it to me," answered Grey Ears. "Perhaps we should do something to say thank you to her!"

"Perhaps we should indeed," agreed Brown Ears. "Hold on right there!" He dashed out of the door.

While Brown Ears was away, Grey Ears busied himself with putting away all the food that they had been given. By the time he had finished, the pantry and store cupboard were both full to bursting.

Shortly afterwards Brown Ears returned, armed with a beautiful, big bunch of flowers. "Let's take these over to Rosie Rabbit as a thank you present," he suggested. "We've just got time before tea."

"Good idea!" said Grey Ears, and the two rabbits set off.

Rosie Rabbit was very impressed with the flowers. "These are quite beautiful, my dears!" she exclaimed. "It was lovely to hear such good news about you two today, I must say! Come in and have your tea with me before you go back home. I'm making mushroom surprise and apple turnover!"

The two rabbits did not hesitate. The very thought of such a delicious meal made their mouths water, and the food they had at home would keep.

Much later, after a lovely evening at Rosie's, the two rabbits were back home and preparing for sleep.   They had eaten a great deal at Rosie's but had still found room for a small snack before they settled down for the night.

"What a super day we've had!" cried Brown Ears. "We've got enough food to keep us going for weeks.   I wish we'd thought of this before!" Crumbs from Mrs Duck's apple pie flew from his lips as he spoke.

"It has been good, hasn't it, Brown Ears?" sighed Grey Ears contentedly. "But we must try hard now to keep those resolutions that we made.   They were promises after all!"

Brown Ears put his plate aside and was just about to snuggle down

under the sheets when Grey Ears suddenly had a thought.

"By the way, Brown Ears, where did you get those flowers?"

"What flowers?" asked Brown Ears.

"You know perfectly well what flowers!" said Grey Ears, frowning.

"Oh, yes, those flowers!" said Brown Ears, slowly sitting up in bed. "Well," he said, grinning gleefully "I went down to the allotments, and while Harry Hedgehog was busy showing Deirdre Dormouse the list of our resolutions, I just slipped behind his back and picked a few of his choicest blooms!"

"*Brown Ears*!" exclaimed Grey Ears. "I despair of you! Is there no chance of your changing your ways?"

What do you think?

Burning Ambitions

Old Sam Squirrel's sweet shop was a delight. It sold everything sweet and sticky that you could possibly imagine. Grey Ears loved to go in just to look around and see all the goodies and dream about what he would buy if he had the money. One cold autumn morning he was doing just that, when Sam Squirel asked him, "Why do you come in here so often when you hardly ever buy anything?"

Startled out of his daydream, Grey Ears gave a little jump.

"Oh–um–I just like to look, that's all. I can't really afford to buy anything at the moment. In fact, I can't often afford to buy anything, Brown Ears and I hardly ever seem to have any money, but this time I can't afford to buy anything because we're trying to save up to buy fireworks. It'll soon be Guy Fawkes Night, and we want a really good display." Grey Ears looked a little wistful - "These humbugs do look good though!"

It was Grey Ears'' lucky day. Sam Squirrel was in a good mood.

"I'll tell you what, Grey Ears," he said, "I have to go out on business for a little while tomorrow afternoon. I was going to shut up the shop, but perhaps you and your friend can help me out. If you both mind the shop for me while I am away, I shall pay you with a bag of humbugs and a box of fireworks."

Grey Ears was beside himself with joy. Humbugs and fireworks? It was a dream come true!

"I'll be back after lunch tomorrow!" he squeaked, and rushed off to find Brown Ears.

Brown Ears, too, was delighted when he heard the news that night. But one box of fireworks didn't seem like quite enough for the really wonderful display that he had in mind.

"We still need some more money, Grey Ears. And if we're working all afternoon in Sam's shop we can't earn any money anywhere else, and it's Guy Fawkes Night tomorrow night! We need a plan!"

Grey Ears looked concerned. Brown Ears thought hard for a moment and then beamed.

"I have the very idea, Grey Ears! A penny for the Guy! That's what people do, after all, isn't it? They make a dummy to burn on the bonfire, a model of Guy Fawkes, and before the bonfire they show it to people to earn money to buy fireworks. We must do just that! We'll take a Guy to Sam's shop tomorrow, and it can earn money for us

while we are working."

"But we haven't time to make a good Guy!" protested Grey Ears. "These things are difficult to make!"

"You have a point there," agreed Brown Ears, "but what if I was to tell you that we didn't need to make a Guy?"

"What do you mean?" asked Grey Ears suspiciously.

"Wait until morning, and I'll show you !" exclaimed his friend.

Grey Ears didn't really want to wait until morning to find out what his friend had in mind, but he didn't have much choice in the matter. Within a couple of minutes, Brown Ears was under the covers and fast asleep.

Next morning, Brown Ears had some hard work persuading Grey

Ears to go along with his plan, but by lunchtime he had talked him into it.   Grey Ears was to be the Guy! As soon as old Sam Squirrel had left the shop, Brown Ears was outside, pinning a notice to the wall:

"A PENNY FOR THE GUY! COME AND SEE THIS
MARVELLOUS LIFE-SIZE DUMMY!"

Poor Grey Ears, meanwhile, got dressed . . . .
"Wow, Grey Ears, you look great!" grinned Brown Ears when he

came back into the shop. "Now just keep your head down so that no one recognises you, and for goodness sake keep absolutely still! You make a magnificent Guy, you know!"

Grey Ears grunted and settled down as comfortably as he possibly could on the hard wooden seat.

He felt a little foolish dressed up in these old clothes. He also felt very hot and itchy! Why did he always get the difficult or uncomfortable jobs when Brown Ears was carrying out his wild ideas? It wasn't fair, really it wasn't! He wriggled a little and scratched his nose.

"*Sit still!*" repeated Brown Ears in a loud whisper.

It did not take long for Brown Ears' notice to draw the attention of passers-by.   Everybody who read it wanted to see this wonderful Guy, and came into the shop.   "What a life-like model!" they all said. "How real he looks – almost alive!"

Before many minutes had passed, Grey Ears had quite a collection of coins at his feet.   Brown Ears gathered them up and put them in his pocket.

"Can I stand up now?" asked Grey Ears.

"No, no!   Not yet!" insisted Brown Ears.   "This is going really well! Even better than I expected!"

Grey Ears settled down reluctantly once more.

All afternoon, people kept popping in to look at him, and bit by bit the two rabbits collected quite a lot of money.

"Terrific! Wonderful! Lots of lovely loot!"   Brown Ears was over the moon.

Eagerly he began planning what sort of fireworks they would buy with all their money when they had finished work later that afternoon.

"Rockets, Grey Ears, don't you think?   Lots of rockets!   I do so love to watch them go whizzing up into the air, and then S*woosh*! B*ang*!" His paws waved wildly in the air.

"And we'll have some sparklers to hold, to write our names in the sky with!" he continued, rubbing his paws together with glee.   "Oh! And what are those ones that go round and round called?"

"Catherine wheels," said Grey Ears flatly.

"And just think, Grey Ears, we'll have all those humbugs to suck while we watch the display!"   Brown Ears was so happy he felt like jumping for joy.

Grey Ears was not nearly so happy, however.   It was all very well to have people admiring him, but some of the things that they were saying were making him feel distinctly uneasy.   "I'm really looking forward to seeing that Guy burning on top of the bonfire!" they would say, or, "What a sight he'll make when he burns tonight!"

The very thought of it made Grey Ears tremble – he was glad that he wasn't a *real* Guy!

And then Drew the Shrew and Mrs Hare came in to have a look, and things began to go seriously wrong. Mrs Hare ordered herself a pound and a half of treacle toffees, and while Brown Ears was weighing them out behind the counter, she turned to give Grey Ears a proper inspection.

"My, oh my, that is the best-looking Guy Fawkes that I have ever seen in my whole life!" she declared. Grey Ears tried to keep still and not to sigh. He had heard all this before and was really rather bored with it all.

Drew the Shrew nodded in agreement. Then came the bit that Grey Ears didn't like to hear: "He's going to make a fine display, sitting on top of the bonfire with fireworks going off all around him!" Nevertheless, Grey Ears kept calm and remained as still as a statue.

But wait – what was Drew the Shrew saying now? "It must have taken you a very long time to build such a big Guy – he really is life-size isn't he? How heavy is he? I'll bet he weighs a ton!" Brown Ears was nodding and agreeing and weighing out the treacle toffees . . . . Drew the Shrew went on: "You're going to have an awful lot of trouble carrying that great monster all the way to the top of the fire, you know!"

Brown Ears nodded. "Yes, yes, I suppose I am," he said. Grey Ears held his breath. He had a horrible feeling that he knew what was going to happen next. It was Mrs Hare's turn to speak; "What we should do is gather a few more people together and do the job now. Brown Ears can't do anything while he's working this afternoon, and it's bonfire time as soon as it gets dark!"

Grey Ears could feel himself beginning to tremble. Things were sounding very bad, very bad indeed! Why didn't Brown Ears do something to help him out?

And then . . . "Oh look!" cried Drew. "There are Bill Badger and
Ricky Raccoon coming along the street ! Let's get them to help us put
the Guy on the bonfire now!"

Grey Ears panicked. He jumped up from his seat, screaming.

"No! I'm not going on the bonfire! You can't do this to me! I'm not
a dummy!"

Poor Mrs Hare just about jumped out of her skin. Drew the Shrew
turned to Brown Ears for an explanation, but Brown Ears was up and
running out of the shop already. "Come on, Grey Ears!" he called.
"Let's get out of here!"

And so it was that the two rabbits spent Bonfire Night at home – no food in the cupboards (their pile of money having been left behind when they fled from Sam's shop) and certainly no fireworks or humbugs from Sam, who was very cross indeed!

Grey Rabbit sat in his chair and sighed. "Well, Brown Ears, I've learned my lesson. I shall never, ever listen to you and your silly ideas again. Never!"

Brown Ears didn't believe him.

Do you?

Chimney Sweeps
And Trouble

Brown Ears was hiding behind a tree watching Mr Badger take a
snooze after his chimney-sweeping work. He was longing to tell his
friend Grey Ears about him so he scuttled off home.

"Hello, Grey Ears!" he shouted. "Come on! Look out of the window and I'll show you something very interesting."

"I can only see Mr Piglet, Mr Mouse and Mrs Turtle walking down the street," said his friend.

"Wait a moment.   Be patient, he'll soon be here!" said Brown Ears, adding, "There goes Mr Badger! He's carrying his tools on his shoulder."

"So, what has Mr Badger got to do with us?"

"Well, a lot! Because we're going to do his job."

"What? Us? But we don't know anything about cleaning chimneys," said Grey Ears who was shocked by his friend's latest idea.

The rabbits were a crafty pair; with their clever and cheeky chatter they had managed to convince the whole of Whiskerton to provide for them without having to lift a finger.

However, it was becoming more and more difficult to trick the villagers, and their endless pranks really were a nuisance.

That day, as usual, they were outdoors looking for adventure but had not found it.   As their tummies were now rumbling, a new idea occurred to Brown Ears, who said:

"It's easy work.   I've seen him sleeping like a log."

"Did you say work?" replied Grey Ears.   "But work frightens you!"

"This will be easy.   You'll see! Tomorrow, when Mr Badger is having his daily snooze, we'll borrow his tools and earn some money. Then we'll put them back where they were, and when he wakes up, he won't be any the wiser."

The next day they did as Brown Ears had said and went through Whiskerton's streets, shouting, "Chimney sweep! Chimney sweep!"

Suddenly, Grey Ears said to his friend:

"What will happen if Mr Badger wakes up and finds his tools have gone?"

"Bah!" said Brown Ears.   "He's such a sleepy head he'll spend the rest of the day trying to remember where he left them."

"Do you really think it's going to be so easy?" repeated Grey Ears.

"Mark my words," answered Brown Ears.

"No, you mark mine, but for now let's see how we go!"

"It won't fail this time.   You can't deny it's a brilliant idea."

Brown Ears kept on calling, "Chimney sweeeeeep!"

Mrs Squirrel heard his cry and looked out of the window.   She saw them and called:

"Gracious! What a surprise! Have you two decided to get a job?"

"Do you need us to sweep your chimney, Mrs Squirrel?" asked Grey Ears very politely.

"I don't know whether I can trust you.   Can you really clean chimneys?"

"Of course! Let us do the job!" Brown Ears quickly replied.

Brown Ears and Grey Ears went into Mrs Squirrel's house and through to the kitchen.

They went wild with joy! There on the table was a large steaming loaf. It was fresh out of the oven and smelt delicious.

In the pantry they could see a large chocolate cake covered with red cherries, and on a small shelf there was a basket full of shiny apples.

Mrs Squirrel was rather short-sighted and had not noticed how jittery the two rabbits were. She told them how she had lit the oven that morning to bake some bread and how there was smoke everywhere. Something must be broken.

Brown Ears had a good look and realised that Mrs Squirrel had forgotten to open the small oven door. It would be easy, but ...

"Dear me!" said Brown Ears. "This is not going to be easy.   It
could take a long time."

Grey Ears, who had also realised that they only needed to open
the oven door, was confused, but he quickly guessed his friend's
scheme and said:

"Yes, yes.   It's one of the most difficult faults there is."

"Hmm! We'll have to light the living-room fire to see where the
smoke comes out," said Brown Ears, wrinkling his nose.

They lit an enormous fire, and after a little while Mrs Squirrel shrieked, "Oh! I can't stand this heat! While you're repairing the fault I'll slip round to visit my friend Mrs Magpie."

Off Mrs Squirrel went, and our two friends rushed into the kitchen. At last they could fill their empty tummies!

When they had eaten their fill, they happily looked at each other and burst out laughing.

"All we have to do now is open the little oven door and put out the living-room fire," said Brown Ears.

When Mrs Squirrel returned and went into the kitchen, she thought a whirlwind had passed through it. Most of her baking was gone, and her apple basket was nearly empty. She put on her glasses to look at the note lying on the table. It read:

"It was a difficult job and we were so tired and hungry that we ate a little of your food. You do not need to reward us, you are such a good cook that we feel well paid."

Brown Ears and Grey Ears were on their way home when Mimi Badger called them.

"Hey, you two! I want you to repair the kitchen chimney for me."

"What a nuisance," thought the rabbits. They wanted to go home for a snooze.

"Sorry, but we're expected somewhere else," called Brown Ears.

But Mimi, who could be very bad-tempered, stood in front of them and blocked their way.

"This job is urgent! If you don't do something to stop my chimney smoking, I shall have to send for the firemen."

Our two friends had little choice but to do as Mimi wanted. When they looked inside the kitchen, they were shocked to see that it could not be fixed as easily as Mrs Squirrel's.

"Do we know how to fix it?" whispered Grey Ears to his friend.

"Shut up!" Brown Ears quickly answered. "Don't let Mimi hear you. Look busy!"

They did the job quickly and clumsily, showering clouds of soot over the cooking pot.

"Quick, Grey Ears! There's something blocking it up, and the brooms aren't long enough to reach it. You'll have to squeeze in and squeeze out at the other end, through the living-room fireplace."

Grey Ears almost fainted when he heard those words.

From inside the chimney, Brown Ears could hear:

"What's this? Thank goodness! I've found the blockage.   It's a loose brick."

"Grab it and come down.   Don't waste time!" shouted Brown Ears.

Grey Ears shot down the chimney so fast that he landed in a huge pile of soot in the middle of the carpet.

"What will Mimi say when she sees this mess?" squeaked Brown
Ears. "And she's got such a bad temper!"

But our two friends did not wait to hear what Mimi had to say.
They ran out of the house and hid up on the rooftop.

But they couldn't stay there all day, so when they spotted Mimi on her way home, they quickly climbed down from the rooftop and ran away.

The two rabbits ran past Mr Cockerel and Mr Fox.   They both
looked disapprovingly at Brown Ears and Grey Ears and guessed that
the two rabbits had been playing another trick.

When Mimi saw what a mess Brown Ears and Grey Ears had made on her new carpet and how all the crockery was covered in a thick layer of soot, she was very annoyed.

Poor Mimi didn't know where to start.   There was so much cleaning up to do, and her husband was due home at any moment, and the two rabbits had ruined the dinner.   They really were a pair of rascals.   Mimi thought that they should be punished for the damage they had caused.

When Mimi's husband arrived home, he tried to console her and helped wash the crockery and sweep the carpet.

"Don't worry, darling.   You'll see how everything will turn out right in the end."

"Yes, yes, but who'll clean up the house?"

Meanwhile, our two friends were safely back home.

"We're well out of that!" squeaked Brown Ears, mopping away the sweat from his brow.

"I'm a real mess!" said Brown Ears, looking at his soot-covered

clothes. "Ha! Ha! Ha!" laughed Brown Ears, looking at his friend.

"Don't you laugh at me! You don't look too good either!"

"All right! Don't get upset, Grey Ears! Thank goodness we got away from the Badgers, without getting our tails burnt."

Everybody in Whiskerton had been fooled by the rabbits' tricks and jokes, but Mimi decided it was high time to call in the police, to teach them a lesson.

Luckily for them, Mrs Squirrel said that her own oven was working better than ever since they had repaired it.

"This time," warned Constable Weasel, "I'm not going to lock you up, but as punishment you must clean Mimi's house."

Mimi decided to make them clean out the coal cellar. She hated it because it was such a dirty job.

That evening, while they washed and combed their whiskers, Grey Ears complained:

"I'm fed up with your ideas! Everything always ends up like this!" he said, scrubbing his dirty hands.

"All right! All right! It could have been worse. At least it was only a dirty job! I'll think of a better idea tomorrow!"

And he probably will!